MOMENTS

Bryan Patton

Dedications

To the lady that makes my heart smile, to the one that I share each and every moment with; my wife! I love you and I always will, remember that.

To the Princess and Prince in my life; the main reason why I cannot stop watching the Disney Channel to this day. You guys are my heart; I would do any and everything for you. Please never hesitate to come to me for anything; I will always be there.

Last but not least to my purpose giver, to the one who watches me who blesses me, who keeps me and loves me even if! Lord there will never come a day in which I will not show my appreciation my love and my faith to you! My moments, my life my family; none of it would be possible without your grace or your mercy. And for that I cannot say thank you enough!

With Love,

Bryan E. Patton

Foreword

Our lives have always been defined by the moments in our lives. The moments that made us cry the moments that made us smile from ear to ear. There were moments that we would love to forget and of course there are moments that we would love to always remember. These are the moments no matter the kind; that will forever shape our lives.

We have the power within us, the power that will help us to determine how we allow these moments to shape our lives. It's totally up to us on we handle these moments. Granted bad moments will happen, but that does not mean your life has to go down the drain. Remember I said that these moments will help us define our lives, not guide them. We have the power to take a negative and turn it into a positive. Believe me we have it in us.

"Moments: Stories that define our lives" is a book that was written not to change your life, but to inspire you to think. Before you can feel change, you have to first know you can change. So enjoy reading this book and I pray it will do something to enrich the moments in your life!

Love and Live your Moments!

Bryan

TABLE OF CONTENTS

MOMENTS

DREAM

MOMENTS

    There I was with my hand still extended out towards the basket as I let the ball out of my hand. With a quick swish of the net, I could tell the ball went through; by the yelling of the crowd. But I could not bask in all the glory of my win; due to the fact as I was shooting the ball; a bullet was piercing my body from behind. Somebody in the crowd, taking a guess; did not want me to win; had shot me as the ball was being released from my hand.

    I could feel the bullet entering through my back and passing some of my organs and exiting out of my chest. As I fell I could see people running to and from me, then with a thud; I was on the concrete with my eyes quickly closing. I could feel my heart beating faster and faster as the blood began to rush out of my chest and back. Pressure was being felt on my chest as I felt my body being lifter from the earth.

As I opened my eyes, I could see a number of people surrounding someone; as I looked closer I could tell that someone was me. By that time paramedics had arrived and I could see them lifting me onto a

gurney and putting me into an
ambulance. As they closed the doors
of the ambulance, a bright light
blinded me and I quickly turned from
the ambulance to see what the source
was. The light grew brighter, but as
it did my eyes adjusted with it. I
could see figures standing around the
light, and I began to hear voices
calling out my name.

At first the voices began to
scare me, but as they prolonged; a
calming feeling went over me. I could
hear my grandparents calling me; I
could hear my friends calling me. The
pain from being shot had left me, and

MOMENTS

I began to feel free. I looked around and noticed that I was indwelled within the light; that same light that I was looking into was now all around me.

I felt a hand caressing my shoulder and tears began to soak my face. I began to feel the ultimate joy that I had read about for so long. I no more remembered how it felt to be shot, and dying seemed just a distant memory. At that moment I was not scared to die, I was ready to witness what the next life held for me. I wanted to see what Gods face looked like, I was ready to say hello to all those I was forced to say goodbye to.

I walked around this new place that I was ready to call home, and noticed I could not recognize anybodies face. I could hear their voices, but their faces were not familiar to me. I just knew when I made to Heaven, I would see all of my loved ones, but that did not seem the case. Fear started to overtake all the joy and happiness that I felt and I just wanted to close my eyes and wake up from this bad dream, but I couldn't. It was all too real. I had been shot; I had died, and now I was stuck in this so-called make believe Heaven.

I began to run, but I was not getting anywhere. Everything that I passed looked the same, all the people looked the same. So I tried to run faster and faster and still I was not getting anywhere; and still I could not recognize anything or anyone. This had to be a bad dream; this had to be some sort of nightmare. Looking down at the hole in my shirt covered in red, I knew it wasn't.

So I stopped where I was, and I dropped to my knees. I allowed the

tears to fill my eyes and a heaviness
began to weigh down on my shoulders.
I did not want to go on, I wanted to
stay there; I was afraid. Then a hand
came and lifted my head and the tears
began to dry. I began to fill the
heaviness around my shoulders being
lifter and the fear left me; I began
to fill joy again. I took hold of the
hand and it began to lead me back
towards the light. As we walked I
could hear the voices of my loved
ones singing, and I was comforted.

Standing in front of the light
the hand spoke in a thunderous but
soothing voice saying; "You are my

child, and I love you so. Do right by others and I will truly bless you."
With that I was led into the light and I awoke in my bed. All that was just a dream, I had never been shot, and I had never died. I had never seen or heard my loved one's voices. I never ran through Heaven, I never felt God's hand on my shoulder. God never spoke to me and I never seen the light. It had to be all a dream, right?

PLAY TO LIVE,

LIVE TO PLAY

MOMENTS

It was five seconds left on the clock, my team was down by one point, and I was having the best game of my life. My line score read, thirty-two points, six rebounds, and six assist. With five seconds left in the game, I was the natural candidate to have the ball in the remaining seconds of the game.

We arose from the bench, sweat beads dripping from our foreheads. The desperation we felt, could be

read from the writings on our faces.
I bent down placing my hands on my
knees, taking an extra breath as I
awaited a cue from the refs. With a
blow of the refs whistle, I faked
left and went towards the ball. The
ball was thrown to me; I looked at
the clock and began to make my move.
I lost my man, by faking right, going
behind my back, placing the ball
between my legs, doing the spin move
and I went up with my left hand.

The ball fell through the net,
and the crowd roared; but was quickly
silenced by the thud from my body
hitting the floor. My teammates and

my coaches quickly ran to my side. I could hear them requesting for me to stand up, but my legs had other plans. I kept telling my body to get up, but my legs wanted no part of it, they refused to move. I could feel my mother's tears lubricating my face as they fell from her eyes.

A short time later, the paramedics arrived, they were whispering words in my ear, but the words were being drowned out by the wails of the onlookers. The paramedics lifted me onto a stretcher and began to roll me out of the gymnasium. I could see hands on my

18

legs, but I could not feel them; all I could feel were the tears that streamed down from my eyes. Thoughts began to race through my mind a about a paraplegic life. How would I get around? Would I be able to play basketball again? I must have thought myself to sleep, due to the fact that I remember awaking in a hospital room, with my parents and girlfriend standing around me.

My mother saw my eyes open and she immediately began to cry. Jill; my girlfriend of two years touched me on the forehead, and asked me how I felt. I told her I felt fine, except that I could not feel my legs. She placed her head into her chest and quickly walked away. I asked what was wrong, but my mother swiftly escorted Jill out of the room. I turned towards my father expecting an answer, but he was too busy counting the specks in the floor.

Why couldn't I find anyone willing to answer my question? Was there really something wrong with me? I began to scream out for answers, I mean I was really making a scene. My father ran to me, attempting to act as a restraint, and hearing the commotion; my mother, Jill, and the nurse ran into the room. Knowing the one person who was never able to keep any kind of secret from me, I decided to play my cards with them.

I looked at my mother and she knew exactly what was coming next. From telling me about my birthday gifts, to where our family vacations would be spent; all it took was a certain look and the secret was gone. I raised both eyebrows, dropped my bottom lip, and forced a tear from my eye. This look always worked, and I could see it beginning to work now. My mother quickly ran to my side, almost knocking my father to the ground in the process.

   She started out talking about
how God does things for a reason, and
that there; the talking about God
part, let me know something was
wrong. For instance the time when she
told me God lost his dog so he wanted
to use mines, or the time when she
talked about Grandmas cookies and how
everyone on earth loved them so much,
that word got back to God and he
wanted Grandma to live with him, so
she could bake them everyday for him.
She kept on babbling about God and
why he does things, and it got to a
point where I could not take it

anymore, I had to interrupt her. Just then the doctor was making his way into the room.

I turned to the doctor and asked him, what was going on. He looked around the room at my parents; as if to get their permission, they nodded; then the doctor grabbed my charts and began to tell me about my problem. I began to zone out when he told me, I might not be able to walk again. A steady flow of tears started to fall from my eyes, as I listened to the doctor describe statistics about the people that begin to walk after this type of injury.

MOMENTS

I could not believe this was happening to me, what did I do to deserve such a fate? Was it something I did as a kid? Was it that time, I accidentally stole that pack of gum from the corner store, of was it the time I found that twenty dollar bill hanging around in mamas purse? I refused to believe that God was holding a grudge against me; I just refused to believe God would not forgive me for my childish wrongdoings. I began to pray at that moment, for the strength and determination I would need to get through this time.

MOMENTS

Every morning after breakfast, I would roll myself into the therapy room. I was so determined to walk again; I would lift myself up and practice walking. Of course the first few times, the nurses would find me on the floor, but my will and determination never let me give up. I was holding onto those bars, slowly moving each leg, dragging them along as if they were one hundred pound sand bags.

One day while eating lunch in my room, the doctor came in wanting to speak to me about my progress. I felt I was doing better than expected, but

MOMENTS

I never thought anyone else was noticing. The doctor went on telling me that I would be able to go home on Saturday. He told me for the next two days, to continue with my schedule and on Saturday before I went home; he would lay out another schedule. As the doctor left the room, I began to lie back in my bed and I thought about where I was almost five months ago, and where I am now.

According to statistics, I am not supposed to be going home in two days. According to statistics, someone with my injury is supposed to be lying in some hospital with no motivation at all. But I was

different; I felt I was here to prove

all doctors and statistic keepers

wrong. My doctor and nurse could not

believe how well I was doing; they

could not understand where my

strength was coming from. I was

discharged at about eleven in the

morning, and after riding in the

wheelchair, picking up medication, I

was ready to go home. My doctor gave

me my physical therapy schedule and

sent me on my way.

It had been about five months,

since I had slept in my room. And boy

did it feel great just to be able to

sit on my bed again. Just to be able to look around my room, felt wonderful. I know my injury was not life-threatening, but it sure woke me up like it was. Shattering my knee into pieces was the cup of coffee that I needed to wake-up. I don't know if I ever thanked God or had him on my mind before, but at that moment, God was on my mind.

Praying became a necessary part of my rehabilitation. With each rep I lifted, I could feel Jesus with me; with each slow step I took, I could feel the Lord walking right beside me. It was exactly like they

described it in church, at that
moment I found out that God would
never leave me, nor forsake me. God
was there from the moment, that I had
the basketball in my hand and went up
to take that fateful shot. God was
there when the paramedics carried me
out the gym and into the ambulance.
God was there when I first found out
that there was a possibility that I
might not walk again. Then God was
there when I decided that I was going
to go ahead and live my life no
matter the cards I had been dealt.

I had never felt so strong, as I
did at that moment. It had been I

would say about three months since I
was home from the hospital and after
working as hard as I have been during
this rehabilitation period; I felt I
was ready to go play basketball
again. I had been walking around the
block with my father for about two
weeks now, and every time we make
that journey around the block, I
cannot help but think about all those
people that said or thought that I
would never walk again. Now look at
me; here I was walking, and not only
walking, but feeling as if I could
begin jogging now. With God's help I
was proving all the non-believers

wrong.

One Sunday while the preacher was speaking on the topic of making the lame walk; and I could not help but place myself in the sermon. The lame in the scripture reminded me of myself so much. I was at a low-point in my life, and it was known that there was a possibility that I would not walk. Then to hear in the scripture that Jesus was able to make this lame person walk. I knew it was only God that made me walk again. I left church that Sunday, a better person, a more satisfied and grateful person.

MOMENTS

I had never been on a basketball court since that day I was carried off of it, so I decided to go and see my team play a game against our cross-town rivals. When I walked into the gym, it just felt weird. I imagined that my first time back would be a little less flamboyant than it was. I stepped into that gym and it seemed as if everyone knew I was coming. Almost simultaneously from the young to the old in that gym stood up and gave me a standing ovation as I walked to my seat. I could not believe it; I could not believe all the love that everyone was showing me. I personally wished that they would have been applauding me while I was on the court, but this would do. I felt tears begin to well up in my eyes, and the overwhelming love I got, just made them all pour out. After the game, I could not thank my team enough; they were always there for me. And I could not wait until I was back on the court winning games with them.

That visit made me want to work out even more; I became even more determined than I was before. On our journeys around the block, I convinced my father to start doing a light jog, rather than walk. Soon my legs felt strong enough, and I began to run full out sprints around the block. On some days, you could see neighbors standing outside their houses waving and applauding as I ran by them. I could not believe all of the love that everyone was giving me. It was all very overwhelming, and seeing this just made me want to work even harder. I convinced my parents to invest in a home gym, so that I could work out whenever possible.

In three months time I was a whole lot stronger, and I swear; I actually looked a little bigger.

MOMENTS

Basketball season was a month away, and I knew I had to be ready. I continued to everything I felt necessary; the five hundred jump shots, the suicide sprints, the defensive and rebounding drills all had to be done on a daily basis in order for my goals to be met. When it came time for the season to start, I could feel in my soul that I was ready. I ended up having a pretty good senior season. It was good enough; that I actually got recognized by a few Junior colleges. They were not the Universities that I was expecting, but they were the opportunities that God had promised me.

Before deciding on a school, my parents and I took campus tours of each school. All of their basketball programs were great, but this had to be about more than basketball. I almost lost basketball once before and when that happened I had nothing else I could or even wanted to do. But now, I was smarter; if that was going to happen, this time I would have something to fall back on.

We decided on a small school in Arizona, right outside of Phoenix. They had a great Pre-Law program, and with my wanting to be a lawyer since I was younger; this school was just a perfect fit. Before my accident, I had never thought of doing anything other than playing basketball; but since then basketball just served as inspiration to living life. I was given a brand new determination, a brand new chance to live life as God originally planned me to.

I left that school in two years with an Associates degree in Pre-Law. I also left as leading scorer with a full scholarship to play guard for the University of Arizona. That very first game, when they announced my name in front of that sold-out crowd, sent a vibe through my soul, a vibe so strong; I just wanted to let my eyes roll to the back of my head and fall out from behind. Funny thing is, that strong vibe or feeling still did not do it for national championship that we won my second year at Arizona didn't do it. Getting drafted to play for the Spurs in the NBA didn't do it. Even playing in my first all-star game after five years in the league did not do it.

It was my first game back, my senior year in high school that did it for me. Stepping onto that court, wearing that jersey, and everyone including our rivals; giving me a standing ovation is what taught me my purpose. Growing up I always played basketball as if that was my only way to live, but I found out that I did not have to live basketball, but only play it. Now when I go out to teach my kids, I always start out telling them; never play basketball to live, but live life so that you can play basketball. With everything in life; remember, don't play to live; live to play!

My Best Friend

MOMENTS

Senior year, this was the final year of my high school career. Looking back on the years before, let's me know I can stand and be proud of my accomplishments thus far. Being raised by a single mother, in a neighborhood did not give you many options to choose from. You either chose the way of the streets or you chose school; which was hopefully something that could make you become somebody.

I was born and raised in the projects, so the life of the streets seemed a guaranteed destiny for me. But I was determined not to become

the man my father was. And don't get
me wrong, my father didn't leave me
at birth; the only reason I grew up
without him, was because my father
wanted a better life for me and my
mother. He was tired of us
struggling, and he didn't want to
raise a son in hell. So he did what a
lot of fathers did back then; he got
into the street life.

My father got connected with one
of the biggest drug dealers of that
time. I'll never forget his name; it
was kind of funny to me at the time.
But now, now when I think of it; his
name seemed to fit him perfectly.

MOMENTS

They called him Casino, due to the fact that anybody that dealt with him; basically gambled with their lives. He never played around with anyone that tried to play around with him. He once had someone killed for coming late to a pickup; his reason for the killing; he didn't know if they were held up by the police or someone else for that matter. But there was one person that Casino let slide when it came to coming up short with his money and that was Scape; yes Scape was my father.

They called my father Scape, it was short for scapegoat. My father never did anything wrong as he was growing up. His parents kept a watchful eye over him, probably due in part that he was an only child. So whenever Casino would get in trouble, my dad Scape would take the heat; and he would get off with the most a week in jail. And when my father came out; Casino was there ready to throw my dad a little party just to show his gratitude.

We seemed to be living on cloud nine back then and there was nothing or no one that could tell me any differently, or so I thought. My father was on a run for Casino, when

MOMENTS

out of nowhere my dad's car was ambushed by some of Casinos enemies. Since my father had worked for Casino, Casino's enemies became my father's enemies. My father never had a chance, they beat him until he could no longer recognize himself then they snuffed out his life like it meant nothing. To this day, I am still haunted by the sight of my father lying in that coffin. That day I swore to myself that I would never let myself end up like my father did. That day I promised myself, that there was nothing in this world that was going to step in between a better life and myself.

The day after my father's funeral, Casino and his family came to visit, Casino let my mother know that he was going to take care of us and if we needed anything just to let him know. Then he turned to me, pulled me as if to hug me and whispered; Kevin you're like a son to me. With those words I pulled away, you see it was Casino whom I blamed for my father's death. It was for Casino whom my father was making a run for when he got killed; so who else could I blame. When he noticed me pulling away, he grabbed my arm

and whispered forcefully into my ear,
"Boy don't blame me for your father's
death. He made the decision to
provide for you and your mother, it
was that decision that killed your
father, not me." I tried
unsuccessfully to pull away, and
again he grabbed my arm. "Your father
and me made a promise to each other,
that if something happened to one of
us, then we would take care of the
other's family. I have never broken a
promise, and I don't intend to start
breaking them for your behind. Now
you are going to accept my help
whether you like it or not,

understand? I nodded my head, and
with that I began to look at Casino
differently. For the next six months
or so, it seemed as if my father had
never died. We always had food on our
table and the best clothes in our
closets. There was never a day that
we wanted for anything; we always had
what we needed. Casino had kept his
promise to my father.

One day Jackson and I were
playing football outside in front of
my house. Jackson was Casino's son,
he was the same age that I was and we
were as close as brothers. We did
everything together, where one was;

the other was there also; you could not separate us. We loved playing football together, I was the quarterback, he was the wide receiver; nobody could beat us in "Street Football".

AS Jackson was about to go deep, we noticed numerous people running up the street, some were crying and some were yelling. Somebody had gotten killed, and to a kid in my area, a dead body was something to see. We rushed down the street to see, and when we got there and looked over the body I just froze up. Looking down at the body, it hit me; I just lost my

second father in less than one year.
For about a minute or so, I could
only think about myself and how my
mother and I were going to survive;
then that's when it hit me. Jackson
was now like me, he was now a child
without a father. I thought about
what Casino had told me the day after
my father's funeral. About how it was
my fathers decision that got him
killed, and now six months later it
was Casino's decision that turned
Jackson into a fatherless child. It
was that choice of living the street
life that turned a lot of kid's in my
neighborhood into fatherless or even

motherless children.

When I was growing up I never knew what being broke meant, I never had to think about not having what the other kids had. I had everything I could possibly hope for, but after Casino was killed; those days of not knowing turned into days of knowing. I was forced to grow up quick; I had no choice but to become a man. With Casino gone, there was no help for my mother. Casino did not have a bank account; his money was not stored away in some vault. The money he did have, he always kept in a safe somewhere in his house; and after paying for Casino's funeral there was only enough left for his wife and son. This forced my mother to get a second job, and forced me to become a child full of want. My mother tried her best to provide for me, she did everything in her will to make sure all the plans and goals she had for me years ago, would still become a reality. Thanks to my mother's determination, I landed at one of the best high schools in the country.

Kirkland High School was well known for its academics. The school had one of the highest percentages of graduates in the country, not to mention; a top ten varsity football team. For the first time in my life, I was actually without my best friend. The determination that my mother showed for my life, Jackson's mother did not have. I guess when Casino got killed, the thought of having to make money on her own, did not sit well with her.

Instead of her going out and trying to provide for Jackson and herself, she decided that it be best if Jackson went out and worked instead. Dealing with contacts that Casino had before he died; Jackson's mother was able to get her son a job.

MOMENTS

Not some regular job, but a job like his father; working for the streets.

Dealing with school and the football team, didn't leave me with a lot of time to hang with Jackson. The rare times that I did see him, he was busy making a sell, and I was either on my way to practice or I had too much homework to do. This really began to put a damper on our friendship, and basically when I would see him with his new found friends; it quite frankly had me scared. I was too nervous to say anything to him out of fear of him not trying to know some square school kid. To me Jackson was just another kid I had known when I was younger, and who had grown out of our friendship.

My freshman year in high school, I was not allowed to play for the Varsity team, but I was allowed to start on the Junior Varsity team. That year we had the best football team in the city, not only was our varsity program leading the pack in their division, but so was my junior varsity squad. My mother made it to every game that season, and after every game she would remind me of how proud my father was of me. She would reassure me that he was at every game watching me perform my best. Hearing that from my mother, I believed made me play even harder. It brought out a certain determination in my. When my father was still alive, I always made sure he saw me try my hardest to make him proud. And now knowing even though he is not here physically, but in spirit; made me try even harder.

That year my junior varsity team made it to the championship. We were to play this school that was known to have the roughest and dirtiest defensive line in the state. My

offensive line did very good in
protecting me that game. They allowed
me to stay away from the other tea,
long enough to throw four touchdowns
and lead my school to victory that
night. The others school face let
know their hurt and frustration;
while someone in the crowd let his
gun show his. This guy began to shoot
at my schools side of the field,
hitting at least twenty people.
People were running everywhere,
bodies were dropping like rain onto
the ground; it started to get really
out of hand. Now both sides began
shooting at each other, who would

have thought that a junior varsity game would have caused this much violence.

During all this commotion, I began to look for my mother. I tried to scream out for her, but with all the screaming and gun fire; nothing I yelled could be heard. Finally I did see my mother near the parking lot, dropping my equipment; I began to run towards her. Just as I reached her, a guy that played for opposing the school noticed me and yelled out to someone; pointing out that I was the opposing quarterback. My mother and I started to run, and I could hear guns

being fired from behind us. Either
they were bad shots or someone really
did not want to shoot us; because
neither I nor my mother was hit as we
reached the car. When we got into the
car we looked back, and seen the guys
that were trying to shoot at us lying
on the ground. I frantically looked
around the scene, and jumped like a
ghost had suddenly appeared. Jackson
was standing over the guys, and then
he began to run towards our car, I
beckoned for my mother to stop and
wait.

When Jackson got into the car, I
turned towards him and with my teary

eyes I thanked him quietly. That ride back to our neighborhood was a long and quiet one, while my mother did not approve of Jackson's lifestyle; I could tell she was grateful for what he did back there. That night without the both of us admitting it verbally; Jackson and I were now as close as we had been before our fathers were killed.

Every football game that I had after that night, two important fans were in the crowd. Along with my mother, Jackson would make it to every game that I had. I could tell that Jackson was as proud of me as I played this game we both used to

love. It made me remember all those

nights Jackson and I would be in the

middle of the streets as kids winning

the Super Bowl. Those were the days

when kids from other blocks would try

and take our street football crowns,

in which they never could. Looking at

Jackson smile as I won game after

game made me realize that I was not

only playing for myself, but I was

also playing for my father. I was

playing for my mother, I was playing

for Jackson, and at that time I

finally realized I was also playing

for all those kids that didn't have

the opportunity I had. At that moment I realized what my ultimate goal for playing football was. I finally realized why I was given the chance to play this game I truly love in this fashion. Every time I would step on that football field from that moment on; I would not be alone. I planned on bringing my whole neighborhood with me.

When I finally became a senior, my football career had taken off to a level I do not think I was ready for. I was featured in magazines and sport shows around the country as one of the best quarterbacks in the country.

Each time they would interview me, I always showed appreciation for my neighborhood and all the support they had given me. It was the people in my neighborhood that gave me the drive and inspiration to keep going. It was my family and friends that had my back when I was tired and ready to throw in the towel and give up on all that I had accomplished. To these people, the real recognition was due; it was to these people who I owed my success to.

During my senior year, the varsity team made it to the state championship; it was to be televised for the whole state to see. This was something big for me, and I was so excited to have my biggest fans in the crowd there to cheer me on.

The night before we were to leave, Jackson called stating that he needed to come over my house. When he called he sounded very upset so I rushed outside to meet him, I could see something was wrong when he arrived at my house. His face had the same distraught look he had when his father was killed. I asked him what was going on, but he would not say anything; he just stood there looking into space. Then he finally came out and said that he would not be able to go to my football game. I never did ask him why, I guess it's because I knew him. I knew how Jackson was; if he said he could not make it, it had to be something that was very important; something serious. So all I did was grab my football and told him to go deep. That night took us back to when we were younger. That night we won another super bowl, and we gained even more love for each other.

The next day, before my mother and I drove off to the airport; Jackson came running over to my house

with a football in his hand. When he
gave it to me, I noticed a signature
was placed on it. I examined the
football in greater depth, and found
out that Jackson had signed it for
me; he told me it was for good luck
during my big game. That signature
had meant more to me, than if the
whole N.F.L. had signed it. I took
that football with me on my trip and
I looked at it the whole time. To me
the best wide receiver I had even
known signed it for me that day. It
gave me the necessary inspiration I
needed for my game.

　　While I was in the locker room

MOMENTS

waiting for the game to start, my
mother came into the locker room
accompanied by my coach. I could see
her crying, and it reminded me of the
day she found out my father had been
killed. I ran to her hugging her, and
asking her what was going on. She
could not talk, so my coach told me
and I dropped to my knees crying.
Jackson my best friend; had been shot
and killed an hour after I last saw
him. The last thing he told me was
congratulations and he gave this
football. I was just crying; there
was no way I could play now. How
could I play with something like that

on my mind, how could I stay focused when my mind was totally on Jackson?

That's when my coach and my team got behind me and lifted me off my knees. They already knew; they just didn't know how to tell me. They encouraged me to play, and as we all walked onto the field we wore black patches on our uniforms in memory of Jackson. That game had to be my best game I ever played. Every time I threw to a receiver I pictured Jackson and it made me play and throw even better. The whole game I had teary eyes, the whole game I could not stop crying. That game was like winning the street super bowls with Jackson. At the end of the game, I realized we had won, but I could not celebrate. People were running up to me hugging and congratulation me, but there was only one person that I wanted to see, and that was my mother. When I got to her I just lost it. I fell to the ground crying and she met me down on the ground crying along with me. That championship game was the hardest game I had ever had to play. Not because the other team was that good, but because I had lost another fan; I had just lost my best friend.

MOMENTS

The day of Jackson's funeral was very difficult for me, but somehow I got through it. When it was time to view Jackson's body, I put the same football Jackson had given me into the casket. But this time, it had an extra signature on it. I had signed it, and now it read; Jackson and Kevin the Street Super Bowl Champions. That was the first time I had ever signed a football for someone, it felt real good when I finally gave it to him.

I received a full scholarship to play college ball, and when asked what number I wanted to wear; I

MOMENTS

requested thirty. No it was not my
high school number, I wore twelve.
Thirty was Jackson's number, the
number he wore playing in the youth
leagues, and it's also the number he
would have worn if he was playing
alongside me. So from that moment on
Jackson would forever play with me. I
already had my whole neighborhood
along with me on the field, but now I
had Jackson with me in a special way.
Every time I throw a football from
here on out, I will think of Jackson,
my brother; my best friend.

FIRST SIGHT

MOMENTS

I woke up early in the morning
and yelled out loud as I yawned. I
rushed to the shower and got dressed
in a flash. There was something in my
gut that had me feeling something
today would change my life. I checked
my wallet, and realized I did not
have enough change for the bus fare.
It was like I turned into a detective
of some kind, because it was like I
secured a search warrant with the way
I combed through my apartment looking
for enough change to ride the bus to
work. Finding the correct amount, I
bolted out my front door, praying to
God that I had not missed my ride to

work.

I arrived at the bus stop in time to see the last person board as the bus began to pull away from the curb. I could see as the last passenger walked to the back of the bus, turn my way and open the heavens with her smile. I stood there motionless for what seemed a few days, but realized it to be only a couple of seconds as the bus driver honked the horn beckoning me to board the bus.

I thanked the driver by putting my fare in the change machine and giving him a virtual pat on the back.

MOMENTS

As I walked towards the rear of the
bus, I could feel my head turning
from side to side as I; I guess I was
searching frantically for that
heavenly smile.
Nearing the rear, I saw it happen one
more time; I saw the heavens open as
the most beautiful women smiled at me
again. Her smile was the richest
thing I had seen or experienced ever
in my life. Our eyes met as a silent
conversation began. It was as if our
scenery had changed from the back of
the bus to floating amongst the
clouds.

I thought about telling her she

was the most beautiful woman my eyes
had ever wandered upon, but my tongue
had become numb. I wanted so badly to
tell her how she made my heart
flutter throughout my chest, but "do
you ride this bus often", was all my
tongue could muster. I heard laughter
flow throughout the bus; from the
back to the front of the bus; people
were laughing and pointing at my
corniness. I didn't care, I mean why
should I care, when in my presence
was the rarest of beauties.

As I sat down next to her, I
imagined running my hands through her
short-length hair, I imagined myself

whispering in her ear how I wanted to spend the rest of my life with her. I saw us laughing and smiling at each other the whole night of our first date. I could feel the warmth from her smile as she stared at the diamond I was placing on her ring finger. We danced the night away on our wedding night, before retiring to begin our honeymoon.

Our life together was like that of a Disney fairytale romance. The two kids; a boy and a girl just completed the feelings that we shared. The trips together, the massages we shared as a couple. Those times where we danced, staring into each others eyes in our living room. The times I would sneak up from behind her and kiss her gently on her neck. For all the times when one simple kiss from her would solve any argument we ever had, I wanted to tell her thank you for allowing little ole me to share a lifetime with her.

Sitting on this bus, next to this beautiful rarity, I felt compelled to tell her how I felt. I gathered the courage and I stood to my feet prepared to tell her of my feelings. Standing over this jewel, gazing into her eyes made a lump form in my throat. In one moment, I went from a man full of confidence to a child in need of his mother.

I did not realize how much I had choked until I saw the bus pull away from her destination and her walking into my memory. I got to work that day full of regret, but for some reason; I was still smiling. For the first time in my life I could actually say that I was in love. Some might doubt it; some might question it, while some others will just accept it. It doesn't matter how anyone really feels, I know I was in

MOMENTS

love and I guess you can say that it
was truly love at first sight.

FATHER'S DAY

MOMENTS

Today was my fifty-fifth birthday and my son was coming to visit with his family. He and his wife just gave birth to a son of their own. This would be the first time my wife and I had seen our grandson. Needless to say we were very excited to see the newest addition to our family and his big sister. I was also excited, because my son kept telling me that he had something that he felt I would love to see. I thought about what it could be, but nothing ever came to mind.

When they arrived, I rushed to the front door as excited as a kid

MOMENTS

was on Christmas morning, almost
knocking over my wife in the process.
I opened up the door and the feeling
of awe took over my body, there on
the other side of the door was my
son, standing with his beautiful
family. I could tell a tear fell from
my eyes, because before it hit the
floor, it brushed gently against my
cheek.

As I stood in the doorway trying
to discreetly wipe my tears away, my
son leans in and hugs me. In his arms
was his son, so I placed my arms
around the both of them, and through
that hug I silently reminisced about

MOMENTS

the first time I hugged my son. My
son was only about fifteen minutes
old when the doctor placed his little
six pound body in my hands. I placed
one hand behind his neck and head,
and the other supported his lower
half. I pulled my son into my chest
and it was like God was conducting a
two person orchestra as our hearts
beat along to the same tempo. I
whispered to my son at that moment,
that I would always be there for him.
And now hugging him again with his
own son, made me take some pride in
how well my son had turned out.

My son was the first to graduate

from college, and I helped him open
his own business. The boy just
continued to make me proud, and to
everyone that had an ear to lend I
would let them know that I was proud
of my son. Now here I stand before my
blessing from God, attempting to tell
him he has done well by me, but my
tears would not let me. I was excited
to see my son and his family, I was
equally excited to see what he had
brought to show me, but here I was
crying. I had to catch myself before
my manhood ran out the door I just
let my family walk through. So I
punched my son in the arm as if to

tell him to stop being a punk.

I grabbed their bags from the porch and rushed them inside before anymore of my manhood crept away. I saw my son about to sit in my favorite chair; I stopped him dead in his tracks, and let him know that although he could not sit there; his son could. So I took my grandson and we sat together in my chair. My son walked over to me with an envelope that looked awfully familiar. As he inched closer I could tell the envelope was in my handwriting, and when he placed it in my hands, I have to admit, and I became spellbound. It was a letter that I had written to my son when he was only fifteen months old.

I looked at him, with the most puzzled look I could muster on my face. "I can't believe you still have it", I told him. He looked at me and told me to read it. "Out loud", I asked. He nodded his head. I opened the envelope and it was like déjà Vu as I slowly displaced the letter from its home. I neatly unfolded the aging piece of paper and slowly became overwhelmed as I began to read.

To my Son,

MOMENTS

I am able to thank God today, for he has answered at least one of my prayers. My prayer was that he'd watch over you as you grew to be a man, and to one day have a son of your own. You see I wanted you to serve witness to the joy and excitement that you brought into my life. Now I will not say that things will be easy and I can't possibly say that it will be hard. But one thing I can say to you is that I promise to always be there for you. My son even if I tried to tell you, I still could not let you know how much you mean to me. And like you're sister you stole my heart away, the day you graced

this world with your presence.

When your mother was pregnant

with your sister, she would

constantly ask if I had any

preference when it came to gender,

and I would quickly tell her that it

really did not matter, just as long

as the baby was healthy. I still felt

that way when your mother told me we

were pregnant again. And let me be

honest, am I glad you're a boy. Every

time I see you strike across the

house with that wobbly run of yours;

I imagine you running through the

park preparing to catch a pass from

me. I'm sitting here watching you and your big sissy play and it brings warmth to my soul. I can't help but smile after all your little body was forced to deal with.

Who would have known that when you were born you would have twisted bowels, and we would not find out until you were six months old and that you would require surgery. My heart dropped further than it ever has the moment the doctor told your mother and me about the procedure. I had promised myself that I would protect you from all harm, and here

MOMENTS

you were in a little hospital bed,

unaware of what was to transpire. I

tried to be strong for your mother,

while she cried the whole time. She

cried when you were transported from

hospital to hospital by ambulance,

she cried when the paramedics told me

that I could not ride along, and that

only your mother would be able to

support you. Your mother and I shared

a couple of tears as the ambulance

drove away from where I was standing.

That's when I began to feel failure

kick in, even though I knew the

paramedics were helping I could not

help but feel that I was allowing my

little boy to be kidnapped by some strangers. And that feeling only got worse as they rolled your bed through the double doors that would not allow any parents. I though I had fainted and was in a coma for at least two days, but realized I hadn't because I was still staring at the doors as they locked shut.

Son I want so much for you, I want you to succeed in every aspect of your life. I want you to be more of a man than your father could ever be. There is so much that I have to show and teach you, and then there will be so much you'll have to learn

92

on your own. But I promise to always be right there for you. Never forget to call yourself a man before you call yourself anything else. And always trust Gods word above anything else.

Loving you always,

Dad

After I read the letter, I just sat there in complete silence staring at my family and we all shared a great big hug; as tears steadily streamed down my face. This had to be the best father's day I could remember having in a very long time.

MOMENTS

Happy Fathers Day!

A SONG

MOMENTS

One day I was sitting in my office working on a story for my magazine when the phone rang, and I received the best news of my life to date. Yes my wife telling me that she was pregnant was a great moment in my life; but this news had to be up there. Daniel Polk, who was being heralded as one of the greatest singers alive was requesting for me to help him write his auto-biography. When Daniel first called, I could not believe it; how could I when people were constantly calling acting as if they were someone of importance. So naturally; I had to question this caller on his authenticity. Much to

my amazement; it truly was Daniel

Polk, and really did require my help

with his story. We must have talked

for about an hour or so, but before

hanging up; I made sure that we set-

up an official meeting date; just to

finalize the outline of the book.

About a week or so later, I

arrived at our pre-determined meeting

spot; totally excited about the

opportunity that I had been given,

but without me knowing; my dream

assignment was going to quickly turn

into a nightmare. I ordered a cup of

coffee from the waitress, and by the

time I asked for my fifth re-fill; I
noticed that either Daniel was
running late (I understand famous
people do get held up), or that he
just was not coming at all. So I did
what any anxious person in my shoes
would do; I placed a call to the
telephone number he gave me. Letting
the phone ring, I'd say about twenty
times (it was really only three), but
I was ready to hang up; when a woman
answered. The story this woman told
me, hurt so much; it was as if
someone was repeatedly striking me in
the chest. I am serious; it really
felt like someone had taken my breath

away with blows to my chest. I could not believe it, I was actually this close, and now that autobiography that I was to write; would now be a biography; Daniel was dead.

I found out through that fateful phone call that Daniel had been sick for some time now. He was diagnosed with Laryngeal Cancer, which is cancer in the larynx; was basically crippling his vocal cords. Day by day singing was becoming harder for Daniel to do. He had to cancel shows after shows, just to garner enough strength to make it through each day. His record label trying to make it easier on Daniel, even pushed back the release date for his latest album; just until Daniel was healthier to promote it.

From the outside looking in; to Daniel's fans we could not understand why he was canceling shows, we were baffled on the pushed back release date for his album. People started to attribute all of Daniels actions to another of our beloved superstars gone selfish. How could they come to any other conclusion when no one was being told that Daniel was visiting the hospital more times than some of the doctors that work there? No one

was being told that Daniel was being
pumped with enough medication to
tranquilize a ravaging lion.

This woman, who I later found
out to be his wife; told me that
Daniel was beginning to feel that the
timeline of his life was slowly
nearing it's end, and that was the
reason why Daniel had come to me.
Daniel wanted his story to be told,
with the richness and the
authenticity it truly deserved. He
constantly told his wife, that he did
not want just anyone to write his
story adding what they felt should be
told. No one wants to live their

lives, and then in the end have it change because someone thought it would sell more books. Daniel wanted everyone to know about everything; the good and the bad. That's what made Daniel an exceptional man, a role model in a sense.

That's why I took it so hard, after that conversation with his wife. I began to feel sorry for myself; I wanted so badly to know the reason why I was being punished. I worked so hard to get to this point, to garner an opportunity just like this one. And when it arrives; it ends just as abruptly as it came. It was like I was in Vegas playing blackjack, losing on every hand that I bet on. What was with these cards that I was being dealt? I tried to live my life in a certain way; in which I would never try to hurt anyone purposely. I tried to treat everyone with the utmost respect, but here I was still being punished for some strange reason.

When I arrived home attempting to tell my wife of my dreadful day, acting like a whirlwind; she quickly put me into my place. I had never before that day heard my wife speak in such a way. I sat there listening to the words that came out of her mouth, and began to understand where this was all coming from. As she finished, I swear smoke vented from the small pores of her forehead. I was looking up at a much crazed version of my wife; it was as if in that moment my wife had become possessed by another side of her that had patiently waited to show its face.

What was I thinking; if it had not been for my wife; I would still be blaming Daniel for dying; which in turn caused me to miss out on the chance of a lifetime. I actually had

MOMENTS

the gall, to be feeling sorry for
myself; when Daniel was forced to
leave behind a wife and two young
children that really needed him. At
that moment, I began to see why
things in my past were always
happening to me, could it be that I
was actually causing them myself? I
used to be the guy that refused to
believe that I caused my own
problems. They always had to be
caused by someone or something, or at
least that's what I thought.

My wife and I were invited to a
memorial celebration for Daniel; it
was basically just for his family and

105

close friends to prepare themselves

for the funeral service. As we

entered the house, where the

celebration was being held; Wendy

Polk; Daniels wife greeted us. Wendy

and my wife instantly hit it off; all

I had a chance to say was, "Once

again I am sorry for your loss."

Wendy looked at me, almost with the

same fire that my wife had when she

tore into my skin with her words.

"Mr. Silverman, the only person you

should feel sorry for is you." I

looked at her with the most confused

look I could possibly muster. She

continued, "Feel sorry that you never

had the chance to really get to know Daniel. Believe me when I tell you Mr. Silverman, he would have changed your life in some way."

Wendy and my wife walked off leaving me standing there; looking as if a dunce hat was hanging from my head. I had been defeated by these two little women, and they showed their victory by the smiles that were plastered on their faces. So with no one in my immediate area to have a conversation with; I began to make my rounds; much like a politician trying to garner up votes. I was attempting to gather up all the information about Daniel that I could. I wanted

to know from the people that were

closes to him, just the kind of man

that Daniel was. Was it really true

that Daniel would buy every turkey

from the supermarket, drive to his

old neighborhood; and hand those

birds out to all who was in need? I

wanted to know exactly how Daniel was

touching people's lives, I wanted to

see first hand the legacy that Daniel

created and now left for those to

follow.

Just walking around and seeing

some of the faces that was being worn

that day; it seemed that Daniel

touched many of lives. Some were crying, others were laughing as stories of Daniel floated throughout the room. I was most curious about this little old lady, sitting in the corner; in which seemed her favorite chair. At first I watched from afar at this little old lady, who seemed to be having a great time serving as storyteller to a number of kids that circled around her. I could no longer take the suspicion, so I slowly made my way towards her; trying my hardest not to make a disturbance. I stood against the wall, as this lady began to speak about her son; Daniel.

MOMENTS

"I remember my little Daniel; his smile, his laughter; I remember him always wanting to perform. Ever since he was four years old, the boy would always be the first to jump up in church and try to sing lead. Sometimes the choir director would have to make my little Daniel cry when she told him someone else would be singing lead. Yes, if you can believe it, Daniel sure was a little cry baby." I chuckled as Daniel's mother sat in that chair speaking of her son.

"When Daniel was five years old, he got his first taste of stardom

when he was awarded the chance of a
lifetime to sing at a Mahalia Jackson
event. Just seeing him up on that
stage with that great smile of his;
singing his little heart out,
honestly made me proud. And if you
were there to see his cute little
outfit you would agree that he looked
so cute in that little suit and his
little bow-tie. I stood there in that
audience looking exactly like the
proud mother that I was. He had such
a hard time dealing with his father's
passing, so it made me ecstatic to
see him doing something he truly
loved."

MOMENTS

Tears began to form in her eyes, and you could see the eyes of the people surrounding her were starting to fill up also. Now that I think about it, as she continued tears began to form in my eyes also. "From that moment on nothing could separate Daniel from the stage. People from all over; from California to New York was requesting for my baby to sing at their events. Now I knew that Daniel would be something special, believe me I did; but I'm just not sure that I was ready for what he was becoming. They had my boy all on T.V; he was on covers of magazine and newspapers.

They even had the nerve to declare Daniel, my baby; the next big thing."

Standing in the corner with tears forming a stream coming down the side of my face, I could tell that Daniels mother was beginning to have a hard time continuing to speak. It was getting harder and harder to do, but she continued on, determined to let these young people know about her little Daniel. "You should have seen the ways they were announcing Daniel. Ladies and Gentleman, please give a round of applause for the ever so dapper, the young and gifted, Little Daniel Polk. All of that to me was so much for a young boy to handle, but not Daniel. Honey Daniel just took it all in, like a true champ. Every moment that Daniel spent on stage, you could tell that he was enjoying it. You could just tell that the stage was where Daniel belonged. And though I was not totally happy about the songs that Daniel had to sing, I was happy that he was able to live his dream and sing. Just to see him on that stage, up there singing his heart out, gave me a feeling, and um, I'm sorry give me a minute please."

That was it; Daniel's mother had

lost it. Wendy noticed her mother-in-law crying uncontrollably, and rushed to her side. People were handing tissue from all sides. Heck I even offered up my brand new handkerchief, with my initials K.J. engraved. I was reluctant, but when Ms. Polk reached out and grabbed it, I felt much obliged to offer it. I left that memorial celebration, with a new understanding on how Daniel lived his life. Looking inside of his life from a fan stand-point, it would be easy to say that Daniel always had it easy. Without fully understanding where a person truly comes from or the type of things that a person had to endure, one could always come to some obscene conclusion. I appreciated Daniel more, after hearing his mother tell stories about the hardships he went through before he was the Daniel we know today.

Daniel called me that day to help him fulfill something in his life that he felt was very important. Even with him no longer around, I still intended for that deal to go through. Daniel was an exceptional performer, and according to all who knew him; an exceptional man. So why not an exceptional story told long after your life is over? That was my plan, and nothing was going to deter me from doing otherwise. Daniel wanted his story to be authentic, and then that's what his story should be.

The day of the funeral, I woke up and felt as if today was going to be a changing moment in my life. Arriving at the church, it became apparent how important this day was going to be. If you ever saw Daniel perform, then you know how his performances touched and sometimes changed people's lives. There were throngs of people in attendance; each one touched by Daniel in some sort of fashion. From celebrities to family and friends, it seemed more arrived for his funeral, than for one of his concerts. I walked in and found a seat to the side of the church, and waited patiently for the service to start. Roughly about five to ten minutes later; the casket of the late, great Mr. Daniel Polk was wheeled in, followed slightly behind by his family.

Everyone in the church stood to their feet as the casket and the family walked in. Some were actually clapping, as others had trouble looking at the casket knowing that one of their loved ones lied inside.

With the casket in its place, and the

family seated in their respective

seats, the pastor of the church

approached the pulpit, and began

speaking to those in attendance.

"Family, friends, and guest, we

are here to give honor and pay

respect to our dear brother Daniel.

Daniel departed from his earthly

body, and was gathered together to

meet the father in Heaven. We all

pray that one day we can take the

same journey that our dear brother is

currently on. We walk around day in

and day out, and we speculate about

our lives outcome, but how many of us here today can honestly say, we know the exact date and time, when we shall depart from our earthly bodies? All we can do is live our lives in the expectation that one day, and I don't know if it be soon or not; but know that one day God will call us home. And whether he uses a disease or not, how we exit is not important, it's where we go after we exit this world that's important. We are all held accountable for our own lives. So live your lives to please God, and not anyone else. With that said, I offer up prayer for anyone willing to be prayed for. Before I close, let me say to the family, hold your head up high, and know that Daniel is fine. His earthly presence is over, but his heavenly one has just begun. Don't feel sorry for Daniel; feel sorry for yourself. Daniel's in heaven, you're the ones left on earth. God bless you all!"

As the pastor of the church walked back to his seat, a couple of Daniels family and friends made their way to microphone. The Pastor approached the pulpit one more time, "out of respect of everyone that would like to speak; please hold your comments to two minutes." A man that seemed close to Daniel in age approached the podium first. I believe I saw this gentleman at the memorial celebration, but I never had the opportunity to speak with him. Needless to say, since I was given the opportunity to write Daniel's story; I was very interested in what he had to say.

This man introduced himself as James Birmingham, a close friend of Daniel. As a matter of fact, next to the wife Wendy, James was Daniel's best friend. Apparently growing up, the two could not be separated. As he ended his introduction of himself ended, he began to speak of how he and Daniel met.

"I remember when I first met Danny; we were competing against each other in one of those local talent shows. There I was up on stage with my group; we had the outfits, our dance steps, were something to see, and then our harmony; to us no other group, professional or not, could touch us. Then this skinny little old kid, whose voice looked as if it would fit a man who was at least a foot and a half taller, and at least sixty pounds heavier; came on stage and blew my group out of the water. I mean all he did was stand in the middle of the stage and sing. No fancy dance steps, no fancy wardrobe; just Daniel in a funny looking suit, with this great big ole bow-tie." Laughter erupts throughout the church, as the image of a little Daniel wearing a big ole' bow-tie flashes in their minds.

"When Daniel first got on stage, all everyone did was laugh at him, but by the end of his song; nobody was laughing, in fact there were a few people crying. Little Daniel had accomplished something that probably

only him and his mother thought
possible; he had won the talent show.
And not only did he win the talent
show, but he won the praise of one of
the greatest music producers of our
time; Mr. Shelby Webb. Shelby Webb
had worked with all of the biggest
singers back then, so to receive your
reward from Shelby was something big.
I can still remember that day when
Shelby actually changed Daniel's
life."

"Ever since that day at the
talent show, I wanted Daniel to be in
my group. I was hounding him, well
actually it could have been defined

more as stalking; but I wanted him in my group. Day in and day out, I was there in his face, until he was willing to hear me out. First my group sung a song, and then like the pro he was; Daniel took over lead, and at that moment our group was formed. But to make it legal, Daniel had to check with his mother; the boss. Daniel quickly ran home, followed not too far behind by myself. We rushed through that door, like two linebackers chasing down a quarterback, and were stopped just as quickly as if a force field was placed to impede us from getting any closer."

All of sudden James became silent, I could tell as he continued to look at the last bed Daniel's body would ever partake; that speaking was proving to be a difficult task. I remember thinking to myself, that I did not want James to stop speaking, I believed that he had so much to teach me about that point in Daniels life. I wanted to know more, I needed to know more, in a sense I craved more. I silently begged James to continue, and he must have heard me, because he stepped back to the podium, and continued to speak on his friend.

"Sorry about that, now let me see where I was at, okay I remember. When we ran into Daniel's living room, we were stopped by the sight of Shelby Webb standing right in the middle. After their brief meeting at the talent show; Shelby; almost on a continuous basis was constantly briefed on a young man named Daniel Polk. Shelby felt compelled to see for himself just what all the excitement was over. Shelby was standing in Daniel's living room to hear him sing, he wanted to know firsthand, if Daniel truly was, "the next big thing".

"Daniel began to sing, and his mother and I stood there with the biggest grins on our faces; for we knew all Shelby had to do was hear Daniel sing, and the rest would be history. But as Daniel finished, Shelby sat in his seat speechless for a moment. The rest of us looked at each other trying to figure out what was running through Shelby's mind. Did he enjoy what Daniel's voice, did he like the choice of song that he sung? All of a sudden Shelby stood up from his chair, and began to walk towards the front door. Daniel's

mother turned to Shelby, attempting
to get his attention by calling his
name, but Shelby just kept on walking
right out the front door. We were in
total shock, I just stood there
feeling my bottom lip hit the floor,
and Daniel just ran to his mother's
arms."

"I thought Daniel had done a
great job singing, but apparently his
voice wasn't what Shelby had wanted
to hear. Then the doorbell rang, and
Daniel still had his head buried
inside his mother's arms. I looked at
Daniel's mother and she beckoned for
me to open the door; Shelby Webb was

standing there. Daniel looked up, wiping his tears away; still unsure of Shelby's thinking. Shelby looked around at everyone, and then looked at Daniel and proudly proclaimed; "Daniel my boy I hope you're ready. "And with that, Daniel was on his way." "To this day, I still cannot believe how fast everything took off. Daniel and I grew to be very good friends, and he invited me along for his musical journey. I began singing background vocals for Daniel, and during this time; I learned so much about him. I learned about the things that brought him happiness, and I even found out about the pain he persistently tried to hide. I remember the day Daniel finally told me about his father."

This was great, this was the kind of news that I needed to hear. I always wondered about Daniels father, and now was my time, I was about to find the answer to a great mystery. "Daniel said he was about four or five years old when his father was killed. Daniel told me one day his father was coming home from doing some Christmas shopping, when out of nowhere; three men with ski mask jumped out from behind the bushes and shot his father. His father died, right there in the shopping center parking lot. I could see the hurt in his eyes, as he recalled a memory I'm sure he wished was just a nightmare. He said they never caught the shooters, and deep down he probably thought the police never cared."

"Daniel used to say that whenever he sung a song, he would think of his father, and hearing Daniel sing; you could hear the emotion in each note. Hearing Daniel sing was like therapy for the soul. All of your problems seemed to fade away whenever Daniel's voice was heard. Now that I think about it, singing was like therapy for Daniel's soul. Daniel was forced to witness a tremendous amount of pain early on in his life, a whole lot more than most people put together."

"One performance that sticks out the most to me was when we at this church rally. The church wanted Daniel to sing this one song in particular, to this day I cannot remember the song what song they wanted, but whatever the song was; Daniel blew their expectations away. The tears those people shed that day, just could not be explained. Whenever

MOMENTS

Daniel sung in a church, he sung as if his life depended on it. Everybody there was blown away, including his supporting cast. We were supposed to be singing and playing behind Daniel, but Daniel ended up singing all by himself; no music and no background vocals, just him and his audience. I tried to join in that day, but the emotions ceased all sing-a-longs that day. Whatever it was, whether God or his father, the feeling was too strong to do anything else, but enjoy."

James became silent again; he just stood there glancing at the casket, and then staring into the sky. He went back and forth continuously for about a minute or so, and then he cleared his throat and began to sing. James was caught up in the emotion of losing his best friend; the way he sang from his heart was evident on the faces of all in attendance. I could see the pain from losing a loved one and the excitement of God written on everyone's face. I grew up in the church, and that same expression that everyone else had, was written on mines also. I decided not to be involved in church like I used to, and through James' performance, I could feel God reaching out to me. It was as if James had somehow channeled Daniels spirit, and Daniel decided to take one more encore.

As James walked away from the podium, that feeling still had a hold on him. James could no longer speak; God had officially taken complete control over the funeral services. James could do nothing but slowly walk away from the podium, and find his seat amongst the other grieving parishioners. I looked around the church and could not find anyone that was not being touched. Looking into some of the eyes, you could see the hurt of losing a loved one; being lifted as God was working. God had somehow erased the pain from every ones heart. It became evident that Daniel was going to have a joyous home-going.

This reminded me of when my brother died; I was probably about five or six years old. My brother and his friends were playing near these railroad tracks, running up and down the tracks acting as if they were trains themselves. Just then a train was approaching; the engineer blew the train whistle attempting to alert anyone in the way of the incoming

train. One of my brother's friends

got caught up in the tracks, and my

brother went to go help. As my

brother help release the friends

foot, the train was right upon them,

and my brother was killed instantly.

At his funeral, I can see how hard my

parents were taking it. It was hard

for me too, but I cared and worried

about my parents more than I did

myself. I don't remember exactly what

I said, but I do remember grabbing

the microphone, and talking directly

to my parents. Needless to say my

brother had an upbeat funeral

service; yes we cried and were sad even to this day, but for that one day; that one day we celebrated for my brother.

A young girl I recognized from the memorial celebration approached the podium next. She was one of the kids that were seated next to Daniel's mother. She introduced herself as Danielle the oldest of Daniel's two kids. Danielle's younger brother Daniel Jr. made the decision to stand next to his older sister. Daniel Jr. looked to be taken his fathers death pretty hard; during the whole funeral his head was buried

within his mothers arms. Danielle,
though crying seemed to be able to
hold things together. She began to
speak about what her father meant to
her.

"My father was one of the nicest
people you would ever meet; and never
did he have anything bad to say to
you. He always met you with a smile
and a good word. And boy did he smile
a lot, as a matter of fact that's all
my father did was smile. We always
talked about my father because of
that. I mean every time you saw my
father, the man had a smile on his
face, and he would even smile when he

was mad. Boy am I going to miss my father, I just still cannot believe that he is gone. My dad meant so much to me, whenever someone would bother me at school, my dad was there to give me the hugs that made me feel better. My dad was everything to me, what do you expect; I was his princess."

Everything I could ever want I had, I even had the things that I didn't know I wanted. Growing up, my father had me believing that I actually was a real princess. That feeling only lasted until someone at my school told me differently. I could not believe it, but that's how my father made me feel. Whenever mama would say no; sorry to say mama, but my dad would sneak behind her back and give me whatever it was I wanted. Ever since I could remember that's how my dad was, my father was just that kind of man. His family meant everything to him, there was never a day he went without telling us how much he loved us. Even when my dad was death bed, barely able to breathe; and he had the nerve to be checking to see how we were holding up."

"I can still see that day when

MOMENTS

my mother told me that my father
would not be with us much longer. I
was totally upset at him, I mean I
could not believe it. The man told
me, that he would always be with me;
he said that he would never leave me.
So when I saw him lying in that
hospital bed, I just became enraged.
I got mad at God, I got mad at my
daddy, and I even got mad at myself
for not loving my dad enough. I used
to think, if I had listened more;
that he would still be alive. I'm
sorry daddy; I didn't mean to yell at
you." Danielle runs to the casket
yelling and screaming out for her

father. Wendy with Daniel Jr. in tow comes running up to console Danielle. The church could do nothing but watch as this mother who had just lost her husband; was left to console the two kids they shared. With a kid at each side, Wendy approached the podium.

"Hello everyone if you do not know who I am by now, I am Wendy Polk; Daniel's wife. I can still remember the day that Daniel and I first met. It was my senior year in high school; I had just attended the winter ball with a group of my friends. None of us felt the need for dates, so we all decided to go solo together. After the ball; feeling hungry, we all decided on a local restaurant for a little something to eat. Here we are in this restaurant feeling like a million dollars, when we actually see these guys enter the doors."

"Taking a second look, we noticed that it was Daniel Polk and his entourage, we were stunned to see Daniel walk through those doors. To us he had too much money to be eating in a place like that, but I guess everyone gets hungry. Everyone loved Daniel and his music; and some of his biggest fans were sitting across the restaurant from him. A couple of us decided to walk over to Daniel's table, and introduce ourselves. As we approached Daniels table, I noticed that he was watching us the whole time; and then he smiled. That's when I lost it; I kept on walking right past Daniel's table straight into the ladies room. After about a minute or so of me being in the restroom choking myself, one of my girlfriends ran in saying something about Daniel wanting to see me."

"I took another minute to gather myself, fixing my hair and make-up one last time. I opened up the door,

not paying attention ran straight
into Daniel; I was so embarrassed
sitting on the floor, looking up at
my dream. We ended up sitting at a
table of our own that night. It
seemed like days had rolled by as we
sat talking and getting to know each
other. That night Daniel introduced
me to his world; he invited me in and
I gladly accepted. After about two
years of dating, Daniel requested for
me to share this world."

The love that began at that
little restaurant blossomed into a
love that produced these two little
angels. I am thankful to Daniel for

allowing me into his world, and I am grateful to God for Danielle and Daniel Jr., because whenever I look at them I will forever see my husband. Now I see all of you passing the tissue box around, listening to me tell my story about my husband. But let me tell you, the Polk residence was not always the fairy tale romance you are accustomed to. You see my husband was a performer; he was a performer before he met me, and he was a performer during our marriage."

"Daniel would make me so angry sometimes, it was like Daniel loved

performing more than he loved me; I
mean I actually felt that way for
awhile. Don't get me wrong, I am not
saying that Daniel was cheating on me
with another woman, but what I am
saying is that Daniel cheated on me
with his music. Sometimes writing a
new song took precedence over simply
watching a movie with me. And I know
that Daniel loved me, believe me I
do, but sometimes it was just hard
trying to compete with something you
know you could never defeat. Daniel
tried his best to let me know I was
and will always be his number one,
even though sometimes it didn't work;

needless to say he did try."

"I remember the last night we shared together; it was right before Daniel got really sick. It was our anniversary and we had decided to spend a nice quiet evening at home by ourselves. The kids were away with Daniel's mother, and I decided to cook him a meal to rival the best chefs in the world. We sat down to a candle-lit table and reminisced over dinner about the course of our relationship. That night reminded me so much of our first meeting in that little restaurant. And once again we just talked and gazed into each others eyes. That night on our anniversary, we were re-introduced to each other, that night we became even more the best of friends."

"After dinner, my husband led me into the study, that's where we kept the piano; Daniel's favorite room. On top of the piano were a dozen roses, a pillow and a bottle of champagne. Daniel helped me to the top of the piano, where he laid my head onto the pillow, and he sat down and began to sing me the most wonderful song. I promised Daniel that night I, that I would never forget that song; and to this day I hum myself to sleep with it every night."

"Daniel told me that night, that
I was his song. He told me I was his
reason for singing and if I could; I
would tell my husband how much I love
and adore him. That night, that last
anniversary we shared will forever be
embedded into my memory. I want to
say to my husband in front of
everyone here; Thank you baby for the
memories, I thank you for the time we
spent together. Thank you honey; for
allowing me the opportunity to share
this part of your life with you. I
thank you for our kids; I thank you
for our love. And until that day when

MOMENTS

I finally join you, I will forever
remember our song; I'll see you when
I get there."

Wendy walked away from the
podium with her two kids by her side,
to a round of applause and sighs. She
walked right over to Daniel, bent
over touched his hands, and kissed
him on the lips. Watching this made a
number of people cry out as they
watched the final scene of this love
story. With that final kiss, Daniel
and Wendy's romantic love story had
ultimately come to an end. A fairytale to some, inspiration to others;
no matter what was felt about their

relationship, pain was felt when that final kiss was viewed.

The pastor approached the pulpit to deliver the final words over the service. "Before we convene to say our final goodbyes to our dear brother, I have something special that Daniel requested to be played at his home-going; he said it's dedicated to his song." The pastor passed a package on to one of his assistants who quickly had it delivered to the audio section of the church. First a hiss came over the loud speaker, and then we heard Daniel's voice. While listening to

MOMENTS

the tape my eyes begin to swell up
with tears, and my throat soon got
that clogged up feeling. Honestly it
was a touching moment.

    "Hey kiddo, I just wanted to say
one final thing, before I departed
this life. I know I cannot be there
in person anymore, but in spirit
please know that I will always be
there for you. If you ever get
lonely, just remember that last
anniversary night we shared; I hope
it gets you through. I love you
kiddo!" I looked at Wendy and she was
just smiling as Daniel continued to
speak.

MOMENTS

"One more thing before I go; do you remember this song?" A piano began playing and Daniel started to sing a song. Everyone in the church turned their eyes towards Wendy; who just so happened to have her eyes closed. I found out at a later date that the song Daniel recorded for his funeral was the same song that Daniel sung for his wife on their last anniversary shared together. One can only begin to wonder what was going on in Wendy's mind as that tape was being played. She looked to be smiling and crying all at the same time.

MOMENTS

When the tape had stopped playing, and Daniel's voice could no longer be heard; the entire church stood to their feet applauding Daniel for the very last time. Sitting not too far from the family, I could hear Daniel Jr. softly say; "you hear that daddy, all of this if for you. I hope you can hear us." Wendy, Danielle, and Daniel Jr. approached the casket one more time to say their final goodbyes. With a final kiss from each, the three headed out of the church with tears flowing from their eyes. Soon the rest of the parishioners took their turns viewing

Daniel for the last time. Daniel had meant so much to so many people, and for these people just to say goodbye, to an idol, a friend, was the finishing touches they required.

When the last parishioner had viewed the body and exited the church; the pallbearers closed the casket, and the curtains on Daniels story had fallen. It seems to some that as quickly as it began for him, it quickly ended. A tremendous amount of people feel that when Daniel died, a part of the music industry died with him. Daniel brought a gentleman feel to the whole industry, when he sung romance was the feeling of the day. He was known as cupid to a number of fans; due to the number of love connections that were made at his concerts. When you heard Daniel sing, there was never any doubt that he was in love himself. Me personally, I'm going to miss Daniel. Whenever I needed something to say to my wife, one of Daniel's songs would always hit the spot. Daniel will forever be apart of my life.

In our lifetime we all want to do something that we can be remembered for, in hopes of leaving a lasting legacy for our relatives to come. We try our hardest to be the men and women that hopefully our ancestors could be proud of. We all knew a man that surely made his family and his ancestors proud. He was a man of integrity, a man of divine vision. I dedicate this book to a hero of many, and a friend to all. To a man that made the whole world proud, I proudly dedicate this book to a husband, to a father, to the performer, the man; Daniel Polk.